KU-476-258

Published in the UK & Ireland by Alanna Max

This edition first published in 2023

Lenny Has Lunch ©2023 Alanna Max
Text and illustrations copyright ©2023 Ken Wilson-Max
Author and Illustrator Ken Wilson-Max
www.kenwilsonmax.com

All rights reserved. No part of this publication may be reproduced,
stored in a retrieval system, or transmitted, in any form, or by any means,
electrical, mechanical, photocopying, recording or otherwise
without the prior written permission of the publisher
or a licence permitting restricted copying.

British Library Cataloguing in Publication Data available on request

Illustrated with acrylic
Typeset in KGHappy

www.AlannaMax.com

Printed in China

ISBN 978-1-907825-36-1 PB
123456789

Lenny Has Lunch

Ken Wilson-Max

Alanna Max

Mummy's at work. Lenny and Daddy are in the Kitchen.

Daddy's making lunch with vegetables. There are potatoes, an onion, a tomato, a carrot, a leek and pasta.

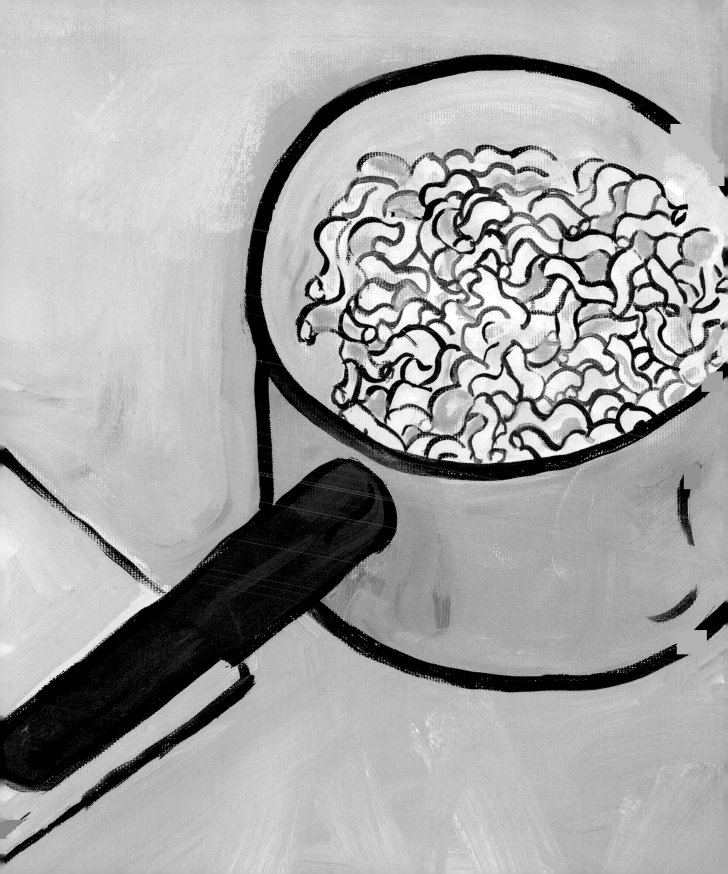

He chops. Chop! Chop! Chop!

"1-2-3 and in the pot!"
Says Daddy.

"1-2-3 and in the pot!"
Says Lenny.

Daddy, Lenny and Wilbur
sing while they wait...

"Row, row, row your boat
gently down the stream.

Merrily,
 merrily,
merrily,

merrily,

life is
but a
dream!"

Lenny points.
Is the food ready?

Daddy says, "Lunchtime!"

Lenny says "Lunchtime!"

Lenny opens wide.
Splash! On the table.
Slurrp! In his mouth.

Splash! Slurrp!
Slurrp! Splash!

Lenny loves yoghurt!
He sucks and spills.

Suck, suck. Plop!

He licks his lips.

"All finished?" Asks Daddy?
"Let's clean you up."

Daddy takes Lenny
out of his chair...

He tickles and tickles.

Lenny's ready to play with Wilbur.